HICCUP

the Seasick Viking

to my father

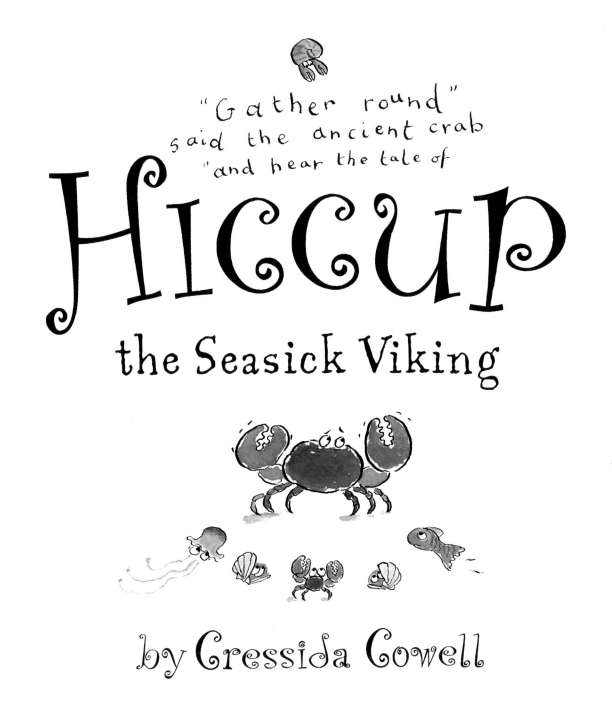

"Gather round"
said the ancient crab
"and hear the tale of

HICCUP

the Seasick Viking

by Cressida Cowell

ORCHARD BOOKS   NEW YORK

Long ago, in a fierce and frosty land, there lived a lonely little Viking, and his name was Hiccup.

Vikings were enormous, roaring thieves with bushy mustaches who sailed all over the world and took whatever they wanted.

Hiccup was tiny, thoughtful, and polite. The other Viking children wouldn't let him join in their rough Viking games.

Hiccup was frightened by spiders. He was frightened by thunder. He was frightened by sudden loud noises.

BANG!

But most of all he was frightened by going to sea
for the very first time . . . next Tuesday.

Hiccup wasn't sure he was a Viking at all.

Hiccup's father was

Stoick the Vast.

Wherever Stoick walked, the ground trembled, flowers wilted, and bunnies fainted. He hadn't brushed his beard in thirty years.

"Only girlie

brush their beards!"

boomed Stoick the Vast.

"Girlies don't have beards," Hiccup pointed out,
but no one listened to him.

And when Hiccup told his father he was frightened
by going to sea, Stoick laughed his enormous Viking
laugh until the salty tears ran down to his enormous,
hairy feet.

"You can't be frightened, little
Hiccup. Vikings don't get frightened."
And he sang the Viking song:

I have blacked the 1,000 eyes

Of a 1,000 angry GALES

Watch me knock the cockles off

The biggest blue-est WHALES

I have given walrus nightmares

Who thought that they were STRONG

♪ marooned a huge typho-o-o-on

On an island off Hong KONG

fortissimo

O ancient prawn-y green-ness

The never-ending SEA

Mess with squirmy jellyfish

But do not mess with me-e-e

O DO NOT MESS WITH ME!

He patted Hiccup on the head and went off to do three hundred push-ups before breakfast.

"Oo, er," Hiccup said to himself. "It all sounds very dangerous."

So Hiccup went to see the oldest Viking of all, Old Wrinkly himself, whose barnacled beard fell down past his toes.

"Your Saltiness," he whispered (for Hiccup was very well-mannered), "do Vikings ever get frightened?"

"Little grandson," wheezed Old Wrinkly, and his breath was like being kissed by mackerel, "I've been wondering about that myself. The sea is full of trials and terrors. But it is also full of marvels and miracles. Go to sea and you can tell me if Vikings ever get frightened."

So, at a quarter to nine on a breezy Tuesday morning,

Hiccup went to sea for the very first time.

At half past nine, Hiccup was wishing he hadn't eaten those two smallish haddock for breakfast.

At a quarter to ten, he was feeling very peculiar indeed.

At half past ten, he wished he was dead.

"I feel
seasick," he
said to his father.
"Vikings don't get
seasick," said
Stoick the Vast.

But this one was—all over Stoick's feet.
Hiccup got sicker and sicker as the storm got
wilder and wilder.

Stoick the Vast sang the Viking song to the storm, but the storm took no notice. A great wave came up and soaked him.

One mighty wave picked up that whole Viking ship as if it were a matchstick and threw it fifty miles to the south. Then one mighty blast from the gale picked up the whole Viking ship as if it were a piece of seaweed and threw it fifty miles to the west.

A terrible black wind howled all over the lonely ocean. It turned that Viking ship upside down and inside out, and sent shivers down every single Viking's spine.

"We're lost," said Stoick, the Not-So-Vast-After-All.

Then a funny thing happened. His face began to turn a greenish hue, and he thought of the thirty-seven largish haddock he had had for breakfast . . . and his stomach began to heave.

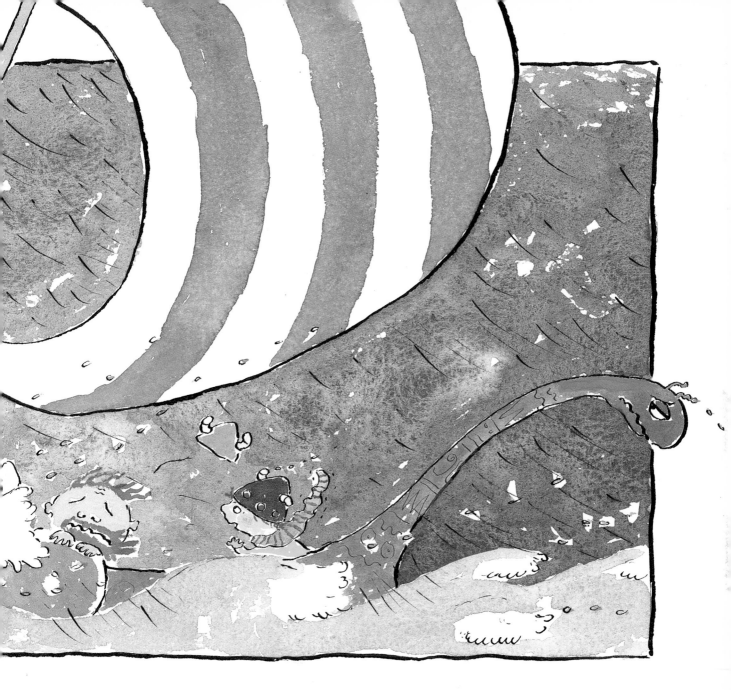

And then all the Vikings turned a pretty green color and all their stomachs heaved, and with an almighty rush they ran to the side. . . .

"Well, well," said Hiccup. "It appears that Vikings *do* get seasick." And immediately he began to feel better. "This direction!" shouted Hiccup.

But the Vikings were too busy
being seasick to steer the boat.

So Hiccup took charge, and a
funny thing happened: the more he
steered, the better he felt.

As he headed for home, that stormy wind filled the sails and the boat skimmed over the ocean at one thousand miles an hour. Out of the depths of the sea came shoals of flying fish with wings, leaping dolphins, and strange whales with horns like unicorns.

There were eels that lit up like lightbulbs and nameless things with enormous eyes that no one had ever seen before—all following Hiccup the Viking as he steered that ship toward home.

"Nice breezy day," hummed Hiccup, steering into the harbor.

"So tell me," said Old Wrinkly, and his old, watery eyes twinkled. "Do Vikings ever get frightened?"

"Sometimes they do," said Stoick the Vast.

"But they get over it," said Hiccup the Viking. "That's what makes them so *brave*."

Vikings ~~Never~~ Sometimes get Seasick

The End

Orchard Books, A Grolier Company
95 Madison Avenue, New York, NY 10016

Printed in Hong Kong
The text of this book is set in 18 point ITC Garamond Light.
The illustrations are watercolor.

10 9 8 7 6 5 4 3 2 1

Library of Congress Cataloging-in-Publication Data
Cowell, Cressida.
[Hiccup, the Viking who was seasick]
Hiccup the seasick Viking / by Cressida Cowell.—1st American ed.
p.   cm.
First published in Great Britain in 2000 under the title: Hiccup, the Viking who was seasick.
Summary: Unlike his large and brave fellow Vikings, Hiccup is small and afraid of everything until he helps steer his ship to safety during a storm.
ISBN 0-531-30278-4 (trade)
[1. Vikings—Fiction. 2. Fear—Fiction.] I. Title.
PZ7.C83535 Hi 2000 [E]—dc21 99-54237